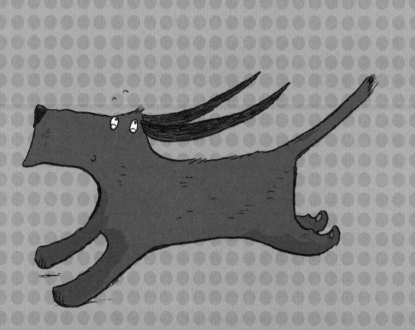

This book is presented to:

_____

This book is dedicated with love
to Missy Harper. You are brave and
beautiful—full of life and adventure.
I can't wait to see what amazing
things God will do through you!

MEET MY
BEST FRIEND

SHEILA WALSH
ILLUSTRATED BY SARAH HORNE

Nashville, Tennessee

I'm bored," Emma announced. "I'm as bored as it's possible for one person to be. . . ."

". . . without self-combusting from absolute total boredom!" Liam agreed.

"Well, why don't you play with Charlie and Wilson?" the twins' mom suggested, pointing at the family dogs.

"They don't want to play," Emma said.

"Aren't you excited about our new neighbors?" their mom asked. "I met them yesterday, and they have a girl the same age as you two. They came all the way from America."

"Wow!" Liam said. "Is that near the mall?"

"It's a little farther than that!" said Liam's mom with a smile.

Ring! Ring!

The twins ran and opened the front door to find their new neighbor. "Hi, I'm Abby," the girl said. "I just moved in next door."

"Hi! Welcome to Scotland! I'm Emma, and this is Liam. We're . . ."

". . . twins," Liam finished. "We have two dogs and a bird and a fish and a chameleon . . ."

". . . and a pony! Well, not a pony, not yet, but definitely all the others," Emma added. "And the dogs do tricks—look!"

"Wow, that's . . . um, amazing," Abby said.

"Would you like to come play in our backyard?" Emma asked.

Abby looked at Charlie and Wilson suspiciously. "Do you think your dogs will like me?" she wondered aloud.

"They'll love you," Liam said. "They've never met an American before!"

"This is our . . ." Liam began.

". . . tree house," Emma finished.

"That is so cool!" Abby said. "I had a tree house back home. My best friend and I used to have our secret meetings up there. I miss my best friend a lot," she said sadly.

Wilson . . . Wilson, wake up. She said "secret" meetings. We may have to investigate further.

I wonder if they'll have snacks?

Abby climbed up toward the tree house. "I bet your friend is hiding up here," she said, peeking into the doorway.

"COLD!" Emma shouted from down below.

"Freezing," Liam added.

"I know!" Abby said. "Your best friend is an animal! Your chameleon? Your bird? Your fish? Maybe another dog?"

"Nope, it's not an animal," said Liam.

The kids headed toward the house. "I bet your best friend is hiding in your room!" Abby guessed. Soon she was looking under all the beds.

"Warmer," said Emma.

"But still cold," added Liam.

Abby started running down the hallway when Emma said, "But now you're very, very warm!"

"Well, you obviously don't keep your very best friend in a closet under the stairs!" Abby said. "I know! I'll check the bathroom!"

Don't mind if I do. I'll be right back, Wilson. Don't let her out of your sight!

A few minutes later, Abby gave up. "That's it. I think you're just pretending you have a best friend," Abby said. "I've looked everywhere!"

"Not quite," said Liam.

"You didn't look everywhere," Emma agreed.

"I looked up in the tree house, inside the doghouse, under the beds, down the hall, in the bathroom, and around the kitchen," Abby said. "The only place I didn't look was in the closet under the stairs!"

"HOT," Liam shouted.

"Boiling hot!" Emma agreed.

"You … keep … your … best … friend … in … a … closet?" Abby asked.

"Come on," Emma said, grabbing Abby's hand. "Come and see!"

"Ta-da!" said Emma, holding out a book for Abby to see.

"Your best friend is a *book*?" Abby asked.

"Not just a book," Liam said. "It's *the* book,"

"It's the best book in the whole wide world," Emma added.

"Then who did God write it to?" Abby asked.

"Everyone!" Emma and Liam agreed. "This is the book that tells us how much God loves us."

"Even *me*?" Abby asked.

"Of course!" Emma said.

"And there's more good news—this friend goes with you wherever you go, even if you move to the other side of the world," Liam added.

"I've never had a friend like *that* before," Abby said.

"The Bible can be your best friend for life!" Emma said.

"For life! And you *don't* have to keep it in your closet!" Liam said with a grin. "We're glad you're our new friend, Abby, but the Bible is really the best friend of all."

Me too.

I do so love a happy ending!

Remember:

Your word is a lamp for my feet and a light on my path.–Psalm 119:105

Read:

Read Acts 17:11–12. These verses tell us about a group of people called the Bereans who were excited to study God's Word every day. Perhaps the Bereans realized that the Bible isn't just a book. It was written by God just for us. And most importantly, it tells us all about God's Son, Jesus, and how much He loves us. If you read and study the Bible like the Bereans did, it can become your guide, your comfort, and, yes, your best friend!

Think:

1. In the story, what do you think it was like for Abby to move away from all her friends? Have you ever had a friend move away?

2. When you first started reading the story, who did you think was Emma and Liam's best friend? Were you hot or cold?

3. Write down a "What Makes a Best Friend" list. Which people in your life match some of the things on your list?

4. The Bible is a friend you can keep by your side no matter where you go. What else makes it a good friend?

5. How does the Bible connect us to Jesus?

6. What are some of the good things that happen when we read and study the Bible?